Jaycie and Her Joybird

By David Isaiah Hamilton

Copyright © 2024

Jaycie and Her Joybird

by David Isaiah Hamilton

Cover Illustration by Ori Endure Hamilton

David Isaiah Hamilton asserts the moral right to be identified as the author of this work.

This novel is entirely a work of fiction. The names, characters and incidents portrayed in it are the work of the author's imagination. Any resemblance to actual persons, living or dead, events or localities is entirely coincidental.

LEXILE®, the LEXILE® logo and POWERV® are trademarks of MetaMetrics, Inc., and are registered in the United States and abroad. Copyright © 2024 MetaMetrics, Inc. All rights reserved.

Library of Congress Control Number 2024913396

ISBN 979-8-9910521-0-8 (Paperback)

ISBN 979-8-9910521-1-5 (Kindle)

ISBN 979-8-9910521-2-2 (Illustrated Hardcover for Libraries and Schools)

First published by Fenix Linn Story Studio 2024

fenixlinn.com

Table of Contents

For my Solita.

For my Ori Bear.

PICTURES
by Me™

This **Pictures by Me** book is designed for you to draw in! That's right. We want you to put your creative ideas right on the pages. Drawing what you read helps to increase comprehension and develop critical thinking skills. You'll love bringing Jaycie and Joybird to life through your very own drawings.

YOU are the Illustrator!

On the following pages, you'll find cool tutorials to help you draw our two main characters. As you read, pay attention to the details in the story and use your own imagination to bring them to life. The special Magic Pencil icon will let you know when it's your turn to make some magic!

 Just look for the Magic Pencil

How to draw Jaycie

① Lightly sketch the shape of Jaycie with a pencil. These guidelines will help us later.

② Start on her chin by drawing a half circle on the guideline. Draw her eyes and nose on the center lines. Jaycie has big hair!

③ Next, finish her cute smile. Then draw her jacket, skirt and legs.

④ Now, draw a cool bow and finish her hair. Then finish her jacket and sneakers!

⑤ Almost there! Add some creative details. Jaycie loves hair ribbons, patches on her clothes and anything else that sparkles.

⑥ Amazing! Now don't forget to add colors. Jaycie loves loves loves lots of colors!

PICTURES by Me

You are such a great artist! Share your drawing with the world and tag us on social media!

   @fenixlinn

How to draw Joybird

① Lightly sketch the shape of Joybird with a pencil. These guidelines will help us later.

② Draw his mohawk first. Then his head, eyes, wing and body.

③ Next, draw his second wing, feet and tail feather. Oh! Now would be a good time to color in his eyes.

④ Now, draw his beak. Start by drawing a triangle for his top beak right on the center guideline.

⑤ Let's fill in the details. Joybird has black stripes on his tail feather, white stripes on his wings, and black feathers around his eyes.

⑥ You did it! Now color him in! Remember, Joybird has magical blue feathers!

Chapter 1

The Artist

Rip! Snip! Tear! Scraps of paper fly through the air, leaving trails of magic hanging there.

The artist is in her zone. The mess. The colors. The texture. She's crafting a creative treasure. A gift. A masterpiece.

The artist's name is Ms. Jaycie Johnson: A third-grader with the brightest eyes, the coolest hair, and the most beautiful brown skin you've ever seen. Many of her neighbors say she is going to be the next great painter, or actress, or rap star, or fashion designer.

Today's outfit is really impressive, adorned with gems and hand-sewn patches of all colors and patterns. Her name is written in bold square letters across her right sneaker. Her left sneaker, which doesn't match the right one, has

4,876 tiny gems glued to it. Her pink glitter shoelaces are untied. Jaycie loves to jazz up her outfits with all sorts of colors and shapes. It makes her feel like a star. A star that everyone can see.

Hey Artist! In this PICTURES by Me book, you get to be the illustrator. When you see this symbol, draw a picture in the frame that shows what is happening in the story.

3

But, if you look around her bed
room, you'll see a true picture of who
she really is. Every wall is covered with
her artwork.

There are paintings of mercats,
and caticorns, and alicorns, and
llamacorns, and ponies, and robot
princesses from the future, a pretty
accurate hand-drawn map of the
solar system, family portraits drawn
in crayon, family portraits painted
with water colors, more drawings
of mermaids and unicorns, and a
really cool collage she made by using

clippings from her big sister's fashion magazine.

Next to her bed stands an impressive mansion playhouse for her dolls, carefully built from Lego bricks and magnetic tiles. It has three levels and hosts parties that are the most popular in all of New Toy City. A pile of barbie dolls, stuffed animals and action figures wait in anticipation for the next big soiree.

Her purple backpack is on the floor next to her desk and her wrinkled math homework is sticking out of it. Now that she has finished

the boring stuff, she gets to let her creativity burst open!

Jaycie is in her zone. Her desk is filled with all sorts of materials. She has construction paper for cutting, white paper for drawing, wooden sticks, ribbons, gems, paint, crayons, flowers from the garden and glue.

It might look like chaos to other people, but she is making something beautiful.

"The magnificent artwork of The One and Only Jaycie!"

Well, that's what Dad used to say when she was a smaller, cuter kid. But things started to change last year on Father's Day.

Jaycie was painting a beautiful mural for Dad. She found the most amazing canvas, in her parents' bathroom, of all places. "This is gonna be the best gift Dad ever got!" she thought, smiling to herself as she made the biggest painting of her art career. She was in the zone, and every few minutes, she would stand back to

admire the way the colors blended on
her canvas.

As she put on the finishing
touches, she took one more proud
look. Eyes big. Head nodding. She was

tapping her paintbrush like a snare drum and rapping,

> Jaycie the Magnificent
> Smart, plus I'm different
> Black girl magic/ Art fantastic
> Got imagination,
> so the world is my canvas!

Jaycie and Dad wrote that together. She raps every time her creative juices are really flowing. "Dad is going to love this one!" she whispered as she started to clean up her workspace. But before she could finish, she heard the door of

her parents' bedroom open. So, she stopped cleaning and quickly slid out to sneak back to her own room.

When Dad followed a trail of empty shaving cream cans and food coloring packets into the bathroom, he let out a big scream. As Jaycie hid in her room, waiting for Dad's surprise, she quickly realized that things weren't happening the way she had planned. She could hear him as he walked toward her room and she started to get nervous.

Jaycie thought her Father's Day surprise was perfect. But instead of saying how much he loved her creativity, Dad scolded her. "Jaycie! You painted on the brand new shower curtain?! Wha- wha- what were you thinking!? It's ruined. Why in the world would you do this?"

Jaycie's heart shrank five sizes. She knew why she did it.

"I worked really hard to paint a picture because I love you," she thought to herself. A million other words and feelings crashed around in her head. Jaycie tried to say them out loud but was never able to get the words to bubble to the surface.

11

Instead, she shrugged her shoulders and mumbled, "Idunno."

Jaycie was so embarrassed. Dad brought her a sponge and cleaning spray so she could "fix this before Mom wakes up." She began wiping off her creativity from the curtain, rinsing the sponge in the sink, and watching the colors swirl down the drain. As she turned to the shower again, she heard a voice behind her say, "Wait!"

It was Joel, her big brother. "What's going on in here?" he asked with a slight giggle.

She replied, "It's not funny!" Sadness swelled in her voice. "I made Dad a painting for Father's Day, but he hated it and said I ruined everything."

Joel stood there in silence for a moment. Then he told her, "I know Dad's upset, but I think this is pretty dope." Joel helped his little sister finish cleaning off the shower curtain and the two worked in sad silence.

Since then, things have not been the same. Instead of making them smile, all Jaycie feels like she can do is make her family angry. Like when she made breakfast in

13

bed for Mom's birthday. She learned that mud cakes don't make great pancakes. Then there was the time she made a fort flag out of her big sister Jada's new dress. Or the time she cut off her dolly's hair and made a cute wig for her baby sister, Janelle. Now, everybody in her family thinks she should just make art "like a normal kid."

Everybody except Joel. Joel is her best friend and the only one in the family who still gets her. That's why Jaycie is so hard at work now. She's making a gift—a masterpiece of a gift. And it has to be the most perfect piece of art ever.

You see, Joel is moving away to college for four whole years! Jaycie is super sad about it. Maybe the saddest that she has ever been. When she thinks about what it will be like without him around, her heart feels like it's on fire. Her brother is her best friend and she's afraid that everything is going to be so much different.

Earlier today, in art class, Jaycie didn't feel like painting with watercolors. She didn't feel like doing anything. She was too sad. Ms.

15

Mitchell noticed and asked, "Hey Jaycie. What's up? You usually love to paint with us!"

"I don't feel like painting pretty things today," Jaycie replied.

Ms. Mitchell paused and then shrunk down to Jaycie's desk. "Can I tell you a secret that only the greatest artists know?" Jaycie can't resist a good secret. She leaned in to hear it.

Ms. Mitchell looked around to make sure none of the other 3rd graders were spying and asked softly, "Did you know sadness can make great art too? Anybody can paint a pretty picture when they're happy. But the happy things aren't the only beautiful things. Using your sadness to make something beautiful, that's what makes you a great artist, Jaycie!"

Ms. Mitchell's words stuck in Jaycie's head for the rest of the day.

"...the happy things aren't the only beautiful things..."

Now, as she sits at her desk, she's using every drop of her sadness to make a very special, top-secret gift for her brother.

Chapter 2
The Prankster

Jaycie is hard at work when a knock on her door interrupts her creativity. It's Joel!

"Heeeey Jaycie," he teases from the other side of the door, "What ya doing in there?"

"Uh, nothing! Go away!" replies Jaycie in a nervous voice.

Joel says, "OK, if you wish."

But instead of walking away, Joel starts to open the door! Jaycie springs up and tries to slam it shut. She laughs. They struggle.

Joel laughs a devilish laugh, like a bad guy in a superhero movie. Jaycie can't let him in! He'll ruin the surprise! She pushes back with all of her might, but he's too strong.

Joel gets the door halfway open, and Jaycie fears that he will see his gift before she is finished with it. But to Jaycie's surprise, he doesn't

squeeze in. Instead, he yells, "Ice Bomb!" and pours freezing cold water on his sister's head!

"Aaahhhhhhh!" she shrieks. A shocked smile grows. "You're gonna pay for that!"

Jaycie chases Joel. Joel runs away howling with laughter. These two are always pulling funny pranks on each other.

They run through the kitchen. Mom gives them a sharp look and says, "Jaycie! Girl, I just did your hair!"

They run circles around Jada while she video chats with her new high school friends.

They run through the living room and Joel jumps right over baby Janelle's car seat. Dad hangs up his keys. They race right by him. He yells something, but they don't hear it. They just run out of the door.

Jaycie finally catches the prankster on the front steps and wrestles him down in the grass. She shouts, "And STILL THE HEAVYWEIGHT CHAMPION OF THE WORLD!" The champ stands towering

21

above her defeated opponent. Then she begins to wipe the cold water from her shirt on her big brother as revenge. The two laugh and laugh.

"I'm gonna miss you, kiddo," says Joel through his smile.

Jaycie's laughter suddenly stops. She sits up and asks him sadly, "Do you have to move so far away? Why would you leave me here with these people? They don't get me anymore."

He smirks and stays quiet for a moment. "I'm only leaving for a little while, but I'll be back."

The thought of her big brother leaving makes it hard for Jaycie to

breathe. As soon as she notices the
teardrop about to fall, she quickly
brushes it from her eye. She's afraid
of what she feels inside. Sometimes
the sadness is like a volcano, and
her tears feel like a pool of hot lava
behind her eyes. She thinks if she
lets the lava fall, it might burn up
everything around her.

Joel puts his arm around his
sister. "Awwww. You're sad," he teases,
"Me too. But don't worry, Sis. Things
will be OK."

Jaycie interrupts, "Nothing is going to be OK!" She breaks away from her brother's hug. "Everything is changing, and I hate it! Jada's always on her phone. Mom is always working now. If Dad isn't at work, he's always holding that new baby. We never play games. Never watch movies. We never even have dance parties anymore. You're the only one who still smiles at me, and now you're leaving!"

Joel's heart breaks for his little sister. "Change is hard," he says in a comforting voice.

Then he pulls out his phone, opens his camera app, and says, "I have an idea. Say cheese."

Jaycie says sharply, "I'm not smiling."

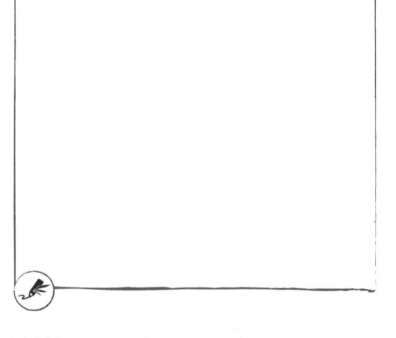

"You don't have to. I'll smile for both of us," says Joel. He stretches his phone up into the air and makes a big goofy smile. Snap. Then he sticks his tongue out. Snap. Then he puffs out his cheeks and closes one eye. Snap. Then he pretends to sniff his little sister, but pinches his nose to act like she smells of stinky cheese. Snap. Finally, Jaycie's frown transforms into a smile. Snap.

"Gotcha!" Joel laughs and says, "I'll print this one and you can keep it as proof that everything doesn't have to change. I'm always gonna be

27

the coolest guy you know." He puts her in a playful headlock and kisses her head.

Just then, Jada opens the door and yells, "Mom says to come in for dinner, nerds."

Jaycie and Joel look at each other and roll their eyes. They do their secret handshake, and tell each other, "Nerds for Life." The two head inside laughing.

Chapter 3
The Tragedy

After dinner, Jaycie goes back to her room to finish her art project. She swings the door open, ready to get to work. But instead of her masterpiece, she finds a clean, empty desk!

"No. No. No. No. NO!" she panics. She thinks Jada must have come in and destroyed it, but her sister has been on her laptop the whole time. Jaycie runs into the kitchen where Dad is washing dishes. She asks desperately, "Dad, did you move my creation?"

Without turning from the soapy water, he replies over his shoulder, "You mean the mess you left in your bedroom. Yes, I cleaned it up. I keep telling you, baby girl, you have to keep your art space clean and neat."

"But I wasn't even done!" Jaycie snaps.

Dad turns to Mom with a confused look on his face. "Who she talkin' too?" Mom shrugs. Dad turns to Jaycie and says sternly, "First of all, watch your tone. Second, you can just make a new one tomorrow." He has no idea how important this is.

Jaycie stands there in shock, trying not to cry. But Dad turns his back and starts washing dishes again. She feels so alone, and the lava might burst out if she doesn't escape right now.

So, she runs out of the house and plops down on the front steps. She buries her eyes in her palms as her hands fill with hot tears.

She's so sad and hates that her favorite person is moving away. And now, she doesn't even have a gift to give him.

Chapter 4
The Rescue

Jaycie sits on those steps, her head buried in her folded arms. Through her sniffles, she begins to hear the distant sound of laughter. Jaycie lifts her head and looks through blurry eyes

Across the street, her neighbors are planting flowers together in their garden. She feels a little jealous and wonders what it would be like to have a different family. Their perfect little family looks so happy in their perfect little garden hats and perfect little rose bushes.

She imagines how she would look in a perfect little garden hat. Before long, Jaycie floats off into a daydream...

daydream

daydream

...here in Jaycie's day**d**ream world things are different, like really different.

It's Saturday morning for the fourth day in a row. Jaycie and her family have just finished cooking sprinkle-filled pancakes covered in powdery sugar.

As they do every Saturday morning, they make their way into the garden. The sky is bluer than the ocean. No. **Pi nk**. The sky is pinker than cotton candy. Four different rainbows cross the sky, intersecting like a busy highway. A Pegasus stops while flying along one of the rainbows and waves to a family of blue jays before continuing on his journey.

Jaycie looks up and **smiles**. She loves it here.

The sights and sounds of her dream garden fill her heart with joy. Maybe it's because the roses smell like **strawberry candy** or because the grass feels as soft as a shaggy carpet. Maybe it's because she can hear the chipmunks laughing as they chase each other up and down the trees.

Or, maybe it's because her **Dream Mother** and **Dream Father** are always here, too. Always smiling. Always fun.

Jaycie adjusts the brim of her garden hat to keep the **purple** sunlight out of her eyes. Her fancy flowing white dress drips with **pink** and red hues. Later today, she will be the flower girl in her auntie's wedding. But not just any old flower girl.

Jaycie will be the most stunning and **beautiful** flower girl in the history of weddings. No flower girl has ever worn a dress tinted by the colors of real flowers from a real garden!

Jaycie is sitting on the edge of the water fountain in her yard. She stares down at her reflection in the pool, smiling proudly. Water shoots up from the fountain like a blooming flower. Even the fish poke their heads out to admire the beauty of her dress.

Dream Mother steps out of the front door and down the porch steps. Jaycie hops up, beaming with pride.

"Dream Mother, Look!"
she exclaims.

Dream Mother replies,
"Yes, Dear."

"I have crushed up your roses
and turned them into dye," Jaycie
explains. "I couldn't bear to wear such
a boring and plain white dress."

Dream Mother's eyes light up
and big red emoji hearts burst forth
like tears of joy.

Jaycie continues, "Your roses
make the perfect hue of pink, and

now I will be the most famous flower girl in history!"

"Oh, Perfect Jaycie," **Dream Mother** sings, "You inspire me. I, too, shall take all of the roses from our garden, crush them up, and mix them with bubbles."

Jaycie smiles in agreement.

Dream Mother continues, "Then I will dye all of our boring white curtains and turn them into pretty pink works of art. What a perfect, perfect idea!"

Dream Mother begins plucking fresh roses from their stems and calls out, "Dream Father, come look at our perfect daughter's perfect creation."

Dream Father appears, and with delight in his eyes exclaims, **"JAYCIE, THE MAGNIFICENT!"**

She bows.

He continues, "You've done it again! Absolutely **brilliant**!"

By now, a huge crowd has gathered in Jaycie's front yard to sneak a peak of her dress. Every person in the entire city... no, every person in the entire state is here.

Jaycie can hear the crowd whisper in **adoration**. She hops up on the edge of the fountain and it turns into a fashion show runway.

The pink sky goes dark and the purple sun becomes a **spotlight**. Jaycie struts up and down the catwalk as thousands of cameras flash.

Click-click-snap. "She's so **perfect**."

Snap-snap. "**Perfect**." Click. "**Perfect**." Snap. "**Perfect**!"

Dream Father stands with the crowd, looking up at his daughter.

He shouts over the commotion, "Oh Jaycie, I am so proud to be your **Dream Father...**

...Dream

...Dream Father...

...Dream father...

The words float off into the air of her daydream. Then, they suddenly get sucked back into her real world.

Jaycie shakes her head, blinks, and rubs the dreamy fog from her eyes when she hears a loud noise underneath her tree. She looks around to see where the noise is coming from. A pile of leaves is rustling and moving on their own. She can't tell what is making the noise. Her curiosity and her fear start to pull her in opposite directions.

Jaycie's imagination runs wild thinking of what it could be. Could it

be a portal to a magical dimension? A dinosaur egg about to hatch? A furry, poisonous spider!? Before she realizes what's happening, she is off the steps and halfway to the sound. Her heart pounds.

With every nervous step, she tries to convince herself, "Turn around, Jaycie." But curiosity trumps fear and pulls her closer.

She crouches down and fumbles around, looking for a stick and never taking her eyes off the mysteriously moving leaves. She takes a big gulp and slowly uses the tip of the stick to clear some leaves out of the way. Her heart pounds louder and louder like a drum at the end of a rock song. This. Is. It...

But then, just like that, her scared frown flips around to a surprised smile. "You were the one making all that noise?" she says.

Sitting in the leaves is a tiny, mysterious bird. It has a little birdie mohawk on the crown of its head, big shiny eyes, and a long black beak. The bird's feathers are all white and gray except for the very tip of one wing. There is one feather on one wing that

57

is a very vibrant blue. The little bird tries to hide it from Jaycie and buries itself again. When she uncovers him a second time, the bird gets scared and hops around in circles.

Jaycie whispers in a soft voice like Mom does at bedtime, "Aww, don't be afraid, little guy. I'd never hurt you."

She slowly gets on her knees and reaches out for him. The scared little bird shrinks back and hides in the leaves again. Jaycie looks around the tree for clues. "Why are you out here all alone? What happened to your family? You must be so scared and lonely."

She can relate. She starts to feel the sadness inside getting hotter and hotter again. "I know how you must feel, little birdie," she says softly. Jaycie gently moves a few leaves so she can see the bird. He is covering one of his wings with the other and looking up at her with scared and sad eyes. "Is your wing hurt?" she asks him. "I can take you back to my hideout and help you get better. Would you like that?"

The bird tilts his head to the side and takes a small hop out from the hiding spot. Jaycie smiles and her sadness starts to turn into determination. She tells the bird, "You're my friend now and things are gonna be OK."

Jaycie looks around for something to carry the injured bird in. When she doesn't find anything that would work, she takes off one of her sneakers and stuffs it with leaves. "This will work," she tells the bird as she gently scoops him up and places him in the make-shift ambulance.

"To the bird hospital!" Jaycie giggles and makes siren noises while sneaking around to the backyard.

Chapter 5
Joybird

"This is my hideout," she tells the little bird proudly. "I built it with my dad when I was a smaller kid. Now, it can be your home." She steps inside and places the sneaker ambulance on a small table.

"The first thing we need to do is figure out what kind of bird you are," Jaycie tells him. She goes into the house and returns with a tablet. "This app will help me. All I need to do is take your picture. Say cheese!" When she snaps the picture, her tablet pulls up information right away.

"Cy-an-o-cit-ta Cris-tata? A blue jay!" Jaycie exclaims. "But... you're not very blue for a blue jay." The little bird slowly uncovers his injured wing to show Jaycie his last blue feather. "Ohhhh, you hurt your wing and you lost all your pretty color. That's no fun at all," she says.

She thinks about what she can do to help. She finds an old popsicle stick and some grass to make a brace for the bird's wing. "Can I hold your wing like this?" Jaycie asks.

She's surprised by how much her bird friend trusts her. She gently ties the popsicle stick to his wing and softly brushes his mohawk. "You're gonna be OK," she says. The bird reaches his head toward her hand for more mohawk petting. Jaycie giggles.

"Do you have a name?" she asks. Obviously, the bird doesn't say anything, but he does tilt his head to the side and look up at her with his shiny eyes. Jaycie smiles and tilts her head like his. Then she tilts her head the other way, and when she does, the bird does the same thing.

"Are you copying me?" she asks. She lifts her right hand and the bird lifts his wing. She makes a funny face and the bird opens his mouth wide, like hers. Jaycie starts to laugh out loud. She stands up to see how far this will go. When Jaycie lifts a leg, her friend lifts his. Then Jaycie gets an idea.

"Dance Party!" she exclaims.

Jaycie takes three steps to the right. The bird does too! Jaycie takes three steps to the left and the bird does too!

Jaycie calls out, "Sliiiide to the right," and her friend follows her movement.

"Three hops this time!" she sings. Jaycie and the bird hop up and down. Then she hollers "Everybody clap yo hands!" before the bird starts clapping his wings and hopping in circles.

Jaycie can't help laughing when he trips over his wings and tumbles over. She plops down full of laughter and joy.

"You're the best bird in the world!" Jaycie laughs. "Even though your pretty colors went away, you're the coolest blue jay I've ever met."

A song pops into Jaycie's head, and she starts to nod to the beat. The bird copies her and nods his head, too!

My Joybird's the best bird
We soar so high
Big wings, big dreams
Do come alive

As she rhymes, something magical comes from Jaycie's smile. She can't see it, but this magic from her smile is swirling above her head. It floats in the room like the sweet smell of freshly baked cookies. More lyrics come to her.

On a mission
Gotta get your blue back again
We can keep smilin'
Even when crying

Magic in the wind
Flyin' wit my best friend
Yeah, magic in the wind
Flyin' wit my best frieeeeeeend!

Jaycie and her Joybird finish the rhyme with their wings spread wide like flying; like just before a hug; like right before taking a bow after a great performance.

"Joybird!" Jaycie shouts. "I'm gonna call you Joybird. Do you like that?"

Joybird tilts his head to the side and Jaycie laughs. As her magic floats in the room, she feels the Joy of her new friendship all over.

It's getting late now and Jaycie has to go in for bedtime. She finds a small toy bin and fills it with leaves. Then she makes a little blanket for Joybird and tucks him in.

"Good night lil' dude," she says, "You'll be safe here. Tomorrow, we're

61

gonna find your blue!" Jaycie gives Joybird a kiss on his mohawk and walks toward her house. Joybird hops from under his blanket and peaks out the window, watching his friend.

As he does, all the magic that Jaycie's smile left floating in the room settles on him like a fresh snowfall. The magic tickles and he flutters both of his wings, hopping around in circles. Joybird's big, bright eyes look happy, and he settles back into his bed to go to sleep.

Chapter 6

The Magic

The morning sun shines into the hideout, waking Joybird from his sleep. All night, the magic from Jaycie's smile has been changing him. If you look close enough, you can see a new sparkle in his eyes. Joybird flutters and stretches his wings.

Inside the house, the same morning sun also stretches through Jaycie's bedroom window and tickles her sleepy eyelids. Only a moment passes before she remembers her Joybird. She springs out of bed, rubs the sleep crumbs out of her eyes, pulls on her favorite rain boots and heads for the back door.

Before she gets there, Dad intercepts her in the kitchen, scoops her up and gives her a big morning kiss. Dad's kisses always make Jaycie's heart fill up, even when she is mad at him.

Dad says, "I made your favorite breakfast" and hands her a blueberry waffle. Jaycie is still upset and wants to tell him how much it hurt when he ruined her creation, but she doesn't have time for that right now. She wiggles her way down and blurts out, "thanksloveyoutoobye."

She enters the hideout holding breakfast and finds the little bird right where she left him. "Hey Joybird!" she says.

Jaycie sets her waffle on the art table. Then, she sits criss-cross-applesauce on the dirt floor, and

begins to inspect her friend. She checks the brace she made the night before.

"Hmmm." Jaycie has no clue how to care for an injured bird. "I bet you're hungry," she hypothesizes. She hops up and leaves the hideout.

While Jaycie is gone, the sweet smell of blueberries floats from the art table across the room and paints the sweetest smell on the bird's nose. Joybird's tummy grumbles and he flutters his wings. I think he wants a bite of Jaycie's waffle!

Just then, Jaycie comes back
with a small shovel of dirt. She dumps
the dirt on the table, uncovers a worm
and dangles it at the bird's beak. But
Joybird doesn't bite.

"Bugs. Maybe you eat bugs!" She pops up and leaves again.

Once more, Joybird flutters his wings. But this time, something truly amazing happens. The blueberry waffle rocks back and forth before it suddenly pops up into the air and begins to float above the plate.

The hungry bird can almost taste the sweetness when Jaycie walks back into the hideout. Startled, Joybird quickly settles back into his homemade bed and the waffle drops back onto the plate.

Jaycie puts a grasshopper on the table. She looks at the bird. The bird looks at her. The grasshopper looks at them both. The grasshopper hops away.

"OK, OK," Jaycie bargains, "If you won't eat, let's see if we can get your color back at least." She inspects him closely. "This is sooo weird," she says, "How'd you lose all of your blue feathers?"

Like a jack-in-the-box popping out of its box, a big, risky idea pops into Jaycie's head. She exclaims, "I

69

got it!" and runs out of the hideout without another word.

Finally! This is it! The poor, hungry bird has his chance. He flutters his wings and the sweet-smelling waffle begins to float again. Inch-by-inch, it creeps through the air. New magic can be slow. But it's so close he can taste it. Just a few more feet...

Bang!

The screen door crashes open as Jaycie runs out of the house being chased by her big sister.

Jada yells, "Stay out of my room!"

Jaycie stumbles back into the hideout. The waffle freezes in midair, but Jaycie is too excited to notice.

"Got it!" she says, out of breath.

Jaycie pulls out some make-up and sits it beside Joybird. She still doesn't notice the waffle floating right behind her. She puts on her artist hat and gets to work.

Puffs of colorful dust fill the space. She is making something beautiful. After a minute, Jaycie steps back. When the dust settles, the bird has a bright pink beak, purple glittery eye lashes, and bright blue wings!

Jaycie looks at her masterpiece. The poor confused bird looks back at Jaycie.

After an awkward pause, Jaycie bursts out in laughter. It's been a long while since Jaycie has had the kind of joy-filled laughs she shares with her new friend.

She finally pulls herself up from the floor. "Sorry, lil' dude. I can't leave you like this. Be right back." Jaycie leaves the hideout to grab a wet wipe, still giggling.

But halfway to the house, her tummy rumbles and she remembers her waffle. She heads back to grab a bite. Right when she gets to the hideout door... she freezes....and you won't believe what her little eye spies!

A FLOATING BLUEBERRY WAFFLE!!!

She stares in quiet amazement and fear as the waffle floats to her

83

bird friend. He reaches up to grab it. Jaycie rubs her eyes in disbelief. Imagine the sight! So many thoughts run through her mind. *Is this bird eating my waffle? Did my waffle just fly? Does my dad make enchanted waffles? What kind of weird, magical bird is this?!*

Then, she whispers aloud, "A magical bird!" When Joybird takes his last bite, Jaycie cracks a small smile and steps inside.

"Bro, did you just eat my waffle?" she asks. "Like, did you make... my waffle... float... in the air? Are you a magical bird?"

Jaycie has to test her hypothesis. She picks up a rock and holds it out to Joybird. "Can you make this move?"

Joybird tilts his head to the side. Then he flutters his wing and the rock shoots up into the air.

Jaycie jumps back and falls to the ground. "Whooooooa! This is the coolest thing in the world! You can move things with your wings, Joybird!"

She smiles, stands up and plucks the floating rock from the air. "It's official! We're best friends forever!" She goes inside to get those wipes.

When she returns, they clean up and dream up all the fun trouble they can get into together.

Chapter 7
The Colors

Jaycie scoops Joybird into her hands and cradles him so no one can see. The two ninjas sneak through the backdoor and hide in the kitchen. Dad is still cooking breakfast, but he is almost finished. As Jaycie crouches under the table, she gets a whiff of those blueberry waffles sitting on the counter. She turns to Joybird, whispering with a smile, "Someone owes me a waffle." Joybird tilts his head and flutters his wing.

A waffle pops up from the top of the stack and heads straight to Joybird. This time, it floats much faster, and Jaycie plucks it right out of the air.

"Aaand whipped cream," she says. Joybird flutters his wing again, and a messy glob of the sweet cream flies out of the bowl but splatters on the table top before it can get to them. Joybird is still getting used to his magic. The duo quickly scampers out of the kitchen before Dad turns around and sees the mess.

After lunch, Jaycie walks through the living room where Mom is cleaning up. Baby Janelle is sitting in her bouncy chair. Classical music plays on the television. Mom asks if Jaycie wants to feed her sister. Jaycie

politely declines. "I'm going upstairs
to play," she says and leaves the room.
But halfway up the stairs, she stops,
crouches down, and pulls Joybird out
of his hiding spot.

"Alright, time to work your
magic," she tells him. The two come
up with their best prank yet. While
Mom is folding clothes, Joybird floats
the TV remote off the stand, and
it drops right in Janelle's bouncy
chair. The baby loves to chew on
things, so she picks it up and starts
gnawing away.

After a few seconds, the television turns from classical music to Janelle's favorite alphabet video. An animated alligator and hippopotamus are on screen rapping:

A is for Apple
B, I'm a boss
C, that's for cookie
D is for my dogs! Woof.

Janelle bounces in her seat to the beat, but Mom stands up to change the channel. She says, "Girl, how'd you get this remote? No more

31

Hippo Hoppigator videos!" Then she puts the remote back on the stand.

Janelle reaches up for her chew toy as Mom leaves the room carrying a big stack of towels. As soon as Mom is gone, Joybird flutters his wings again and gets the remote to Janelle. She giggles with excitement when her favorite rapping animals return.

T is Turn
U is for Up
V is for very, very, very TURNT UP!

The happy baby wiggles, bounces, laughs and slobbers all over the TV remote until Mom comes back and stops in her tracks. "What in the world?!" her Mom exclaims. "I thought I took this from you, young lady." She picks her baby up, turns the TV off, and walks out of the room, whispering to herself, "Geez, I am getting old."

Jaycie and her Joybird giggle, then sneak upstairs to her bedroom to plan their next move.

After a day full of pranks and play, Jaycie and her Joybird hang in their hideout. She is so excited to have a new friend. She picks him up and says, "I'm so happy I found you. I know what it's like to feel all alone, but you won't have to anymore. Neither of us will! As long as I have my Joybird."

Jaycie strokes the one blue feather on Joybird's wing and hums a soft song. He can feel the magic from her care again. It tingles through his feathers and he flutters his wings. Jaycie smiles. Then suddenly, the blue in Joybird's last colorful feather begins to spread! With each stroke, more feathers go from gray to blue. Jaycie is speechless! Soon, Jaycie's Joybird is filled with the most magical shades of blue she has ever seen.

"Now that's a Bluejay!" she exclaims. Joybird flies from her hand and lands on the table. He hops and spins around, then stands in a proud pose. Jaycie scoops him up and hugs her friend. For the first time in a long time, she starts to believe that everything *will* be OK.

Jaycie grabs some paper and markers from her art stash and sits at the table. She begins to draw a picture of herself and Joybird, taking extra time to color in his pretty blue wings. "This is going up on the wall right above my bed, and I'll never take it down," she tells him.

Jaycie is finally getting tired. "The sun is setting. I better get inside before Mom comes looking for me," she says. Joybird hops into his birdie bed. Rubbing her sleepy eyes, Jaycie whispers, "Goodnight, Joybird. See you tomorrow."

Chapter 8
The Masterpiece

Back in the house, Jaycie and Mom read a bedtime story to Janelle. Then Jaycie heads to her room and crawls under her blanket. She stares at the ceiling with a smile on her face, thinking of how much fun she's had with Joybird.

So much fun, that she forgot tomorrow is going to be the worst day of her life! Tomorrow is the day that Joel moves away. Jaycie's sadness returns. She gets even sadder when she remembers that Dad destroyed the gift she was making for her brother!

She buries her head under her pillow to hide the lava leaking from her eyes when she feels something scratchy. "Ouch. What is this?" she wonders out loud.

Jaycie sits up and pulls a photo from under her pillow. It's the selfie that she took with Joel yesterday. He must've snuck into her room and put it there.

Jaycie stares at the photo, comparing her smile to Joel's. She never realized how much they looked alike before now. Even their smiles. Especially their smiles. She stares at her own smile in the photo. Even though she is crying in real life, something about the photo makes her smile, too. It feels weird crying and smiling at the same time, but she remembers something very important that Joybird taught her.

She starts nodding her head to
the beat:

> We can keep smilin'-
> even when crying
> We can keep smilin' -
> even when crying

She wipes her eyes and gets an
idea. Jaycie collects her art supplies,
grabs the photo, puts on her ninja
hat, and sneaks out to her hideout.

Jaycie whispers, "Joybird, are you
sleep?" Joybird pokes his head out of
the little birdie window. She explains

the problem to her friend, then asks, "Will you help me?"

Joybird flies from the window and meets Jaycie at the art table. As the moon rises, the duo gets to work.

They cut, rip, glue.

Paint, sketch, trace.

Glitter! Leaves! Sticks! Mud!

Then, she takes the picture and gently glues it right in the center of her masterpiece. Finally, it is finished. But the moon is setting, the sun is rising, and Joel is leaving soon.

92

Chapter 9
The Gift

Jaycie gives Joybird a fist bump, says bye, and sneaks back into her room to slip under the covers. Just moments later, Mom opens her door. "It's time to wake up, Lady. We need to drop your brother off at the airport." Jaycie is feeling a lot of things

at this moment, yet tired is not
one of them.

Her heart is filled with sadness.
But her sadness is mixed with joy
because she knows Joel will love her
new creation. She gets dressed and
they pack the car for the airport. *I
can't do this alone,* she thinks. So, she
stops by her hideout and sneaks
Joybird into her jacket pocket. Then,
she grabs the box with the gift and
hops into the back seat.

Jaycie rides with her forehead
leaning against the car window
and her eyes closed, as the sunlight

paints red flowers on the inside of her eyelids. Jaycie is so excited and so nervous to give the gift to her brother. But when she peeks inside to check on it, she notices that part of the gift is missing!

She says to herself, "Oh no! Where's the special ribbon? This was supposed to be perfect! I can't give my gift to Joel like this." The morning replays in her mind as she tries to figure out what happened. Her heart rate is beating faster and faster. Her stomach is knotting up tighter than when Dad ties her sneakers.

Joybird peaks out from her jacket pocket to remind her not to worry. But she's sad still and it feels like a volcano again. She's trying so hard to keep the lava inside that she doesn't even notice the car has stopped at the airport.

Joel and Dad get out and grab his duffle bag from the trunk. Joel reaches through the window and rubs Jaycie's head, saying, "I love you, kiddo!" Then he leans in and whispers, "Don't let these people drive you crazy."

Mom says, "I heard that!"

As he walks away, Jaycie still doesn't know if she wants to give Joel an imperfect gift. She's holding back her tears when Joybird peaks out of her pocket again. He tilts his head to the side and her car door unlocks. Jaycie smiles at him. This must be what courage looks like.

Just before Joel walks into the airport, she bravely calls out, "Wait!" Jaycie unbuckles, opens the car door with her box in hand and runs to give him a big hug.

Nervously, she hands him the gift. Joel opens the box and stares at the gift.

Silence. This is taking too long. Why isn't he saying anything? He must hate it. Jaycie's thoughts run wild and turn four seconds into an eternity of silence.

She can't take it anymore and blurts out, "I know it's not perfect. It was supposed to be, but we stayed up all night because Dad threw the first one away and..." The lava refuses to be held back and her tears burst out, running down her face. "...we had a really cool ribbon for you to hang it up, but I must've left it in the hideout, and it's OK if you don't really like it because neither do I and..."

Joel interrupts her, "It's awesome. This is really dope, Jaycie!"

Jaycie sniffles, "It is?"

"Yeah, sis. This is gonna look great in my dorm room. What inspired you to make it?" he asks.

Jaycie wipes her tears and tries to talk through her sniffles, "It's proof that everything doesn't have to change. We made the frame out of sticks from the hideout and we decorated it too."

Then Joel asks, "We?"

"Yeah, me and my Joybird,"
she says. Jaycie pulls Joybird from
her pocket and Joel laughs. A laugh
breaks through Jaycie's tears, too.

"You always surprise me, Kiddo!"
Joel bows and says, "Nice to meet you,
Joybird! Take care of my little sister
while I'm gone."

Joybird tilts his head to the side.
Jaycie interprets for Joel, "He says
'Pleased to meet you.'" The two laugh
a very big laugh, and Joel wipes his
little sister's tears. "Are these sad tears
or happy tears?" He asks.

Jaycie thinks for a second and says, "Both."

They give each other the biggest hug and Jaycie realizes that her tears don't burn as bad when she just lets them fall.

Meet the Author

David Hamilton is a man of many titles: documentary cinematographer, former educator, spoken word poet, proud father of two bright and beautiful girls, dedicated husband and avid pizza maker. Using these experiences along with his incredible upbringing in Buffalo, NY, David brings a unique blend of creativity and insight to his storytelling.

"Jaycie and Her Joybird" is his first published chapter book, inspired by his passion for art and emotional well-being. His focus on his family's needs and dedication to their love shines through in his writing; when you meet his characters, you fall in love with their journey, too.

Fenix Linn Story Studio is a boutique publishing company for young readers. We exist to create, curate, and share stories that inspire young readers to find wonder in the beauty around them. If our mission is successful, there will be a tribe of young readers who love the art of story, the practice of imagination and the discovery of new perspectives so much that their adult worlds will one day be filled with awe-inspiring color and creativity. Imagination and the love for finding new beauty in ordinary things are essential skills for a thriving and fulfilling life. We hope our stories make this imaginative discovery a core love for our readers.

The name Fenix Linn is very near and dear to us. In honor of my late nephew Amari Phoenix and my late niece Maya Lynn, whose lights were taken from our world but shine brightly in our hearts forever, Fenix Linn Story Studio will donate 10% of its profits to organizations working to improve prenatal care, reduce instances of pregnancy and infant loss, and support grieving mothers in such difficult times.

To find out more about the organizations we support, and to donate, please visit fenixlinn.com.

97040981R00066